SWASHBARKLERS of the SEA

Cynthia Kremsner

PELICAN PUBLISHING COMPANY

Gretna 2019

The word "Pelican" and the depiction of a pelican are trademarks of Pelican Publishing Company, Inc., and are registered in the U.S. Patent and Trademark Office.

Library of Congress Cataloging-in-Publication Data

Names: Kremsner, Cynthia, author, illustrator.
Title: Swashbarklers of the sea / by Cynthia Kremsner.
Description: Gretna : Pelican Publishing Company, 2019. |
Summary: Illustrations and rhyming text invite the reader to
    join a pirate treasure hunt on the high seas. Includes
    glossary.
Identifiers: LCCN 2018017031| ISBN 9781455624140
    (hardcover : alk. paper) | ISBN 9781455624157 (ebook)
Subjects: | CYAC: Stories in rhyme. | Pirates—Fiction. |
    Dogs—Fiction.
Classification: LCC PZ8.3.K8689 Sw 2019 | DDC [E]—dc23 LC
    record available at https://lccn.loc.gov/2018017031

Printed in Malaysia

Published by Pelican Publishing Company, Inc.
1000 Burmaster Street, Gretna, Louisiana 70053
www.pelicanpub.com

Come hither, ye seadogs, and listen to me.
I speak of a pirate who taunts this great sea.
His name is Barkbeard. He's fearsome and bold.
He's taken me treasure of emeralds and gold.

He steals in the shadows
and howls in the dark.
His scurvy old dog bite
is worse than his bark.
Nary a seadog's spied him or his crew.
I've set course to change this
and I'm taking you!

It seems that his legend gives you a scare.
But this be his map and me treasure's out there.
Gather your courage, for fortune or fates!
Come, ye swashbarklers. Our destiny waits!

There's bounty aplenty for all,
don't ya know.

Come, ye swashbarklers,
and give a yo-ho!

Where seas begin boiling are hurricanes born.
We're bound for an island by Cape of the Horn.
All paws on deck! No dogpile for us.
Through rainfalls and sea squalls, it's treasure or bust!

Up in the crow's nest, me matey alarms.
He's sighted the menace that dooms us to harm.

Roll
Out
the . . .

CANNONS!

CRASH

Set the sails tight!
Come, ye swashbarklers.
Prepare for a fight!

Now we be as fearsome as he,
don't ya know.

Come, ye swashbarklers,
and give a yo-ho!

He crests a great wave and we lay down our swords.
It's just a wee rowboat, with no crew aboard?
And who could be out there to skipper the course
but a miniature dog and tiny seahorse?

They wash up to our ship on sea swells and surges.
Come, ye swashbarklers. A wee lot emerges!

He's wheezy and queasy
and just a bit soggy.

He bumbles and tumbles
and smells of wet doggy.

Heave ho, me mateys, the captain's been tricked!
For this be not Barkbeard, all seasick and licked.
Get out the nose plugs, me mateys. Pew-*ee!*
Swashbarklers were swindled by a pup of the sea.

"Of course me be Barkbeard. I lost me ol' boat
and jumped in me dinghy to keep me afloat!
I summoned Sea Biscuit to give me a tow.
The waves they did batter and the winds they did blow!"

It seems that ol' Neptune enchanted the weather
and stirred up the sea to bring us together.
A pack is much stronger with more, don't ya know.
Come, ye swashbarklers, and give a yo-ho!

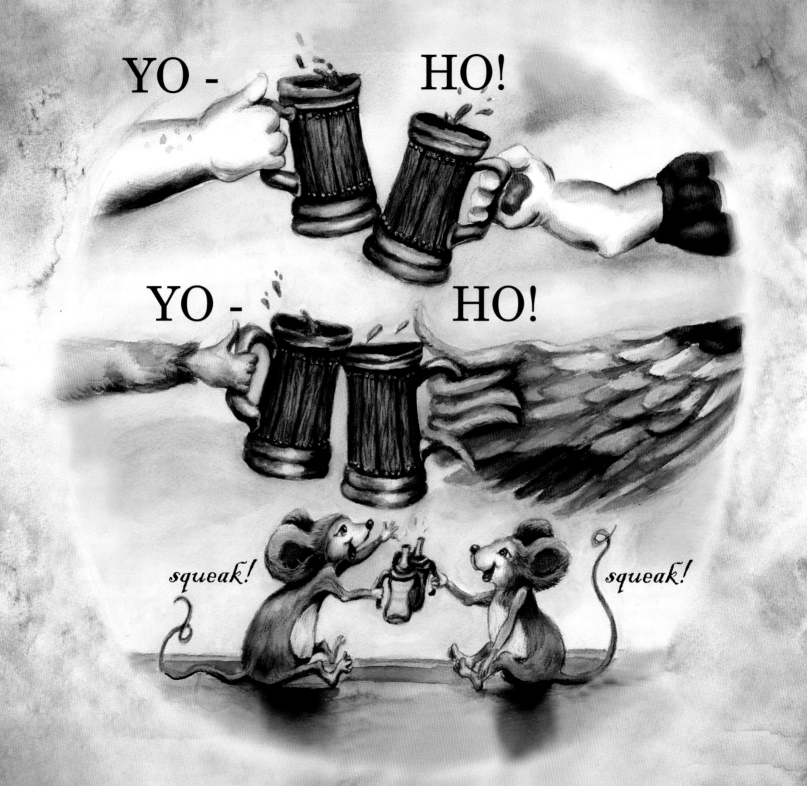

We hoot and we howl at our feared preparations
and join our new friends in great celebrations.

Yo-ho, me mateys, yo-ho, let's go.
We'll share this adventure, 'cause fair wind, she blows!

Thar's treasure in friendship for ye, don't ya know.
So come, ye swashbarklers, and give a yo-ho!

Glossary

All Paws on Deck! (dog version of "All Hands on Deck!")
A command to *"get up here; don't squeal and don't yelp,"*
and a seafarer's call to come swiftly and help.

Barkbeard (doggy double of British human pirate, Blackbeard)
Edward Teach was a privateer, working for the royals.
He fought and captured sailing ships and looted all the spoils.
When Teach became a pirate, his name seemed a wee light.
So it was changed to Blackbeard and readied him to fight.
Queen Anne's Revenge was his ship;
he skippered her with pride—
a warship called a "frigate,"
with masts both tall and wide.
Blackbeard used theatrics to scare his enemies.
He placed lit fuses in his beard . . .
and terrorized the seas.

Bounty
'Tis a bit of a jackpot for hard work and deeds
and a reward to honor
loyal mates of all breeds.

Cape of the Horn (Swashbarkler speak for Cape Horn)
This rocky point near Chile's end,
where east and west seas merge,
is quite a dangerous trading route
when winds and sea swells surge.

Crow's Nest
The best place to survey the seas wide and vast
is this nest-like perch near the top of a mast.

Dinghy
It's a wee little rowboat that gets sailors to land,
because ships are too heavy to push off the sand.

Matey
Be it smooth sailing weather or rip-roaring tide,
this fellow seadog stands strong by yer side.

Neptune
None be as mysterious as this bloke can be.
He's *majestically mighty* (and god of the sea)!

Scurvy
These kinds of seadogs aren't the tail-wagging sort.
They're gnarly and snarly
with tempers quite short.

Seadogs
When rainfalls and sea squalls
put crewmates to test,
these tail-wagging sailors'
skills are the best.

Skipper
A word for all captains
who lead ships and crew.
They be called skippers,
and that's what they do!

Spoils
It's property that's taken
for gain by a brute.
We call that treasure "spoils"
(another word for loot).

Swashbarklers (dog version of Swashbucklers)
A swaggering swordsman
who's gritty and daring;
a land-lubbing daredevil who's also seafaring.

Yo-Ho!
Thar be a chant of sailors, whether hard at work or play.
They give a hearty shout-out, and "yo-ho" is what they say!

YO-HO!
YO-HO!
YO-HO!
YO-HO!
YO-HO!

squeak! squeak!

Friend-SHIP